Dear Parent:

Your child's love of reading starts here!

Every child learns to read in a different way and at his or her own speed. Some go back and forth between reading levels and read favorite books again and again. Others read through each level in order. You can help your young reader improve and become more confident by encouraging his or her own interests and abilities. From books your child reads with you to the first books he or she reads alone, there are I Can Read Books for every stage of reading:

SHARED READING
Basic language, word repetition, and whimsical illustrations, ideal for sharing with your emergent reader

BEGINNING READING
Short sentences, familiar words, and simple concepts for children eager to read on their own

READING WITH HELP
Engaging stories, longer sentences, and la[...] for developing readers

READING ALONE
Complex plots, challenging vocabulary, and high-interest topics for the independent reader

I Can Read Books have introduced children to the joy of reading since 1957. Featuring award-winning authors and illustrators and a fabulous cast of beloved characters, I Can Read Books set the standard for beginning readers.

A lifetime of discovery begins with the magical words "I Can Read!"

Visit www.icanread.com for information
on enriching your child's reading experience.

MOLLY OF DENALI: Berry Itchy Day
Copyright © 2020 WGBH Educational Foundation. All rights reserved.

PBS KIDS® and the PBS KIDS logo are registered trademarks of Public Broadcasting Service. Used with permission. All rights reserved.
MOLLY OF DENALI™ is a trademark of WGBH Educational Foundation. Used with permission. All rights reserved.

MOLLY OF DENALI™ is produced by WGBH Kids and Atomic Cartoons in association with CBC Kids.

Funding for MOLLY OF DENALI is provided by the Corporation for Public Broadcasting and by public television viewers. In addition, the contents of MOLLY OF DENALI were developed under a grant from the Department of Education. However, those contents do not necessarily represent the policy of the Department of Education, and you should not assume endorsement by the Federal Government. The project is funded by a Ready To Learn grant (PR/ AWARD No. U295A150003, CFDA No. 84.295A).

www.icanread.com

ISBN 978-0-06-295044-4

20 21 22 23 24 LSCC 10 9 8 7 6 5 4 3 2 1   ❖   First Edition

I Can Read!

1 BEGINNING READING

MOLLY of DENALI

Berry Itchy Day

Based on a television episode
written by Raye Lankford

HARPER
An Imprint of HarperCollinsPublishers

I'm super excited today
because my family
is going to pick *jak*.
That means blueberries in Gwich'in.

We love to eat blueberries,

and we like to cook with them, too.

So we need lots of *jak*!

"Ready to go, Molly?" asks my mom.
"Thanks for watching the store!"
she says to Tooey.

"Happy to help," Tooey says.

"Don't forget bug repellent!"

I grab the repellent

off the counter.

It will keep mosquitoes

from biting us.

When we arrive at the river,

there are tons of mosquitoes!

"Let's get on the water," Dad says.

"They won't be so bad there."

We jump in the canoe

and start to paddle.

But the mosquitoes follow us!

"Pass the bug repellent,"

says Dad.

Dad sprays the repellent.
"That's odd . . . this smells
like dog perfume," he says.
That's what you spray on dogs
when they roll in something stinky.

Oops . . .

I just sprayed my dog, Suki,

with dog perfume this morning!

I must have mixed up

the bottles on the counter.

We head to shore and make a fire.

The smoke keeps the mosquitoes

from biting us.

The problem is, we can't pick *jak*

if we're stuck by the fire.

We really need repellent!

"My grandmother used to make
repellent from plants.
But I don't know the recipe,"
says Mom.

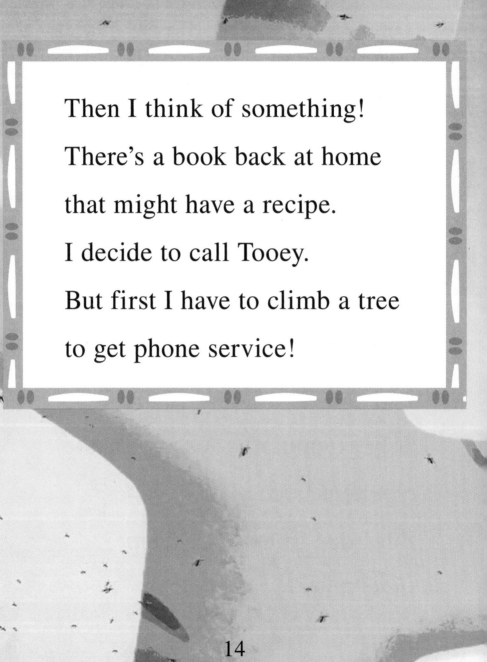

Then I think of something!

There's a book back at home

that might have a recipe.

I decide to call Tooey.

But first I have to climb a tree

to get phone service!

I ask Tooey to find the book.

"I'll call you when I find the recipe.

But here's an idea while you wait,"

he says.

"I heard that elephants

cover their skin in mud

to keep bugs off!"

We decide to try it!

We take mud from the river

and put it on our arms and faces.

But the mosquitoes keep biting us.

"It's time to give up on the berries
and head home," says Dad.
Mom and I stay by the fire
and Dad canoes back for the truck.

Mom sees how disappointed I am.
"We'll try another day," she says.

Just then, Tooey calls.

"Hey! I remembered that
elephants use mud to cool off,
not for bugs," he says.

"No kidding," I say.

While we're on the phone,
Tooey finds the recipe!
We need four plants:
yarrow, stinkweed, marigold,
and wild onion.

Mom and I start to look

for the plants we need.

Tooey sends a picture
of the ingredients to my phone.
We use the picture to make sure
that we have the right plants.

Wild
Onion

We put everything in a bucket.

I take a video of us

making the recipe.

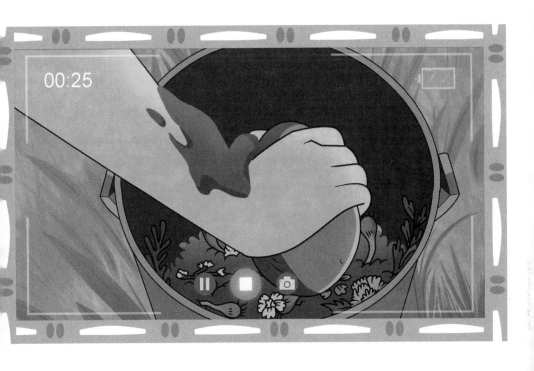

We squish up the plants.

"*Baasee'*, plants," Mom says.

That means thank you in Koyukon.

"Thank you for protecting us

from mosquitoes," says Mom.

After we squish the plants,

we add a little water.

"Time to test it out!" says Mom.

I put the mixture

on my arms and face.

I stand with my arms wide.

I wait to see if bugs will bite me.

But I don't feel anything. . . .

I'm not being bitten!

The recipe worked!

Just then, Dad pulls up in the truck.
It took so long to get the repellent
that it's time to go home.
We'll have to pick berries
another time.
But wait—I see something!

There are blueberries!

Right on the bush by the truck!

I run over and pick a few.

I pick just enough *jak*
to bake exactly one muffin.
My parents and I decide
to split it with Tooey.

"Thanks for watching the store,"
says Mom.

"Let's eat!" says Dad.

Molly's Berry-Picking Tips

Here are some tips for having a fruitful berry-picking adventure with your family!

1. BE SAFE: You may be outside for a while, so be sure to pack sunscreen, a hat, water, and of course, bug repellent!

2. BE PREPARED: You'll need something to put all of your berries in. You can use a basket or a bucket.

3. BE INFORMED: Bring a field guide and ask an adult to help you identify berries that are safe to eat.

4. BE PATIENT: Berries are small, and it takes a while to pick a bucketful!

5. BE GENTLE: When picking berries, gently roll them between your thumb and fingers. They will easily fall off the branch without being squished.

6. BE RESPECTFUL: Leave some berries on the bush so that when they drop to the ground, the seeds inside can sprout new plants. If any berries fall on the ground while you're picking, ask them to grow strong next year!